D1529768

Get set for a magical book
that brings mischievous fairy folk, such as woodland fairies and water sprites, to life.

Fairyland Magic uses augmented reality technology to set loose a range of sparkling fairies, fluttering across these pages in breath-taking 3-D. Here's what to do…

1 Check that your computer has a webcam and that it can run the augmented reality (AR) software on your installation disc (see the **Minimum System Requirements** panel opposite).

2 Put the **installation disc** into your computer and double-click on the installer software. Then follow the on-screen instructions to install the software on your hard drive and start the program.

3 As you go through the book, look out for this symbol which shows you're on a **special AR page**. Once you see that the software is running, hold the page in front of your webcam. Now watch your fairy come to life!

FAIRY-WATCHING TIPS

Look out for special keys you can press to enter Fairyland and make your fairies fly, hover and sprinkle fairy dust.

For a different angle, try turning or tilting the page, or hold it nearer the webcam to get really close!

To view full screen, click the green button on the AR window. To close the window, click the red cross.

For the best fairy animation experience, avoid too much light reflecting off the page.

Make sure your computer speakers are turned up loud!

Need some help?

If you've got a problem, check out our website for troubleshooting information:

www.carltonbooks.co.uk

TO GEORGIA, A FRIEND OF THE FAIRIES

...when the first baby
laughed for the first time, the
laugh broke into a thousand pieces
and they all went skipping about, and
that was the beginning of fairies. And
now when every new baby is born, its first
laugh becomes a fairy. So there ought to
be one fairy for every boy or girl.

Peter Pan, J.M. Barrie

THIS IS A CARLTON BOOK

Design and text copyright © Carlton Books Limited 2010
Illustrations © Patricia Moffett 2010

Published in 2010 by Carlton Books Limited
An imprint of the Carlton Publishing Group
20 Mortimer Street
London W1T 3JW

A catalogue record is available for this book from the British Library.

ISBN: 978 1 84732 579 2

Art Director: Russell Porter
Executive Editor: Selina Wood
Managing Art Director: Lucy Coley
Editorial Director: Jane Wilsher
Production: Claire Hayward

Fairyland Magic

Alison Maloney

Illustrated by Patricia Moffett

MADE WITH MAGIC
AND LOVE
BY CARLTON BOOKS

Fairyland

Did you know that fairies are everywhere – in your garden, in the woods, and even in your house? Fairies live in all countries across the mortal world, but their true home is the far-off kingdom of Fairyland. This magical realm is the birthplace of all fairies.

The Magical Realm

Fairyland looks quite different from our world. The sky can change from blue to green in an instant, and the clouds look like candy floss. The rivers run with shimmering gold and the lakes contain pure dew water. Flowers of every type grow in Fairyland – from roses and violets, to magical blooms of silver and gold.

In the shops, pixies sell fairy food, clothes and shoes alongside fairy dust, wands and ingredients for magic spells. Grocery stores are bursting with honey, dew-drop drinks and fruit, and magical herbs, with strange names like Mouse-ear Hawkweed, Hog's Fennel and Squirting Cucumber. Fairies use fairy gold for money, but beware the fairy that tries to sneak some out of Fairyland – it will instantly turn to dry leaves!

Fairyland is a lovely place to live and, for the most part, everybody gets along very well. Bad fairies are banished by Titania, queen of the fairies, and must be truly sorry before they can return. Those who are exceptionally good are granted a certificate of goodness, the highest honour the fairy queen can bestow.

LEAVING FAIRYLAND

Fairies sometimes leave Fairyland to do good work in the human world. Before travelling they must sign a pledge to stay as far away from human adults as possible. Then they are questioned by the fairy council and are given written permission by the council and the queen. Fairies who leave Fairyland must return at least once a year for the midsummer celebrations. Any fairy who leaves without seeking the queen's permission is banned from returning for seven years.

The Fairy Queen's Castle

On top of a steep hill overlooking all of Fairyland stands a magnificent fairy castle. Here lives Titania, queen of the fairies, and her husband Oberon, the fairy king.

Titania is kind and fair to her subjects. She often throws fantastic parties in the castle's banqueting hall. Dressed in their best gowns and finery, the fairies feast on delicious fruits, berries, nectar and honey. When they can eat no more, they dance in the ballroom, or under the moon in the castle gardens, until daybreak.

You spotted snakes with double tongue,

Thorny hedge-hogs, be not seen;

Newts, and blind-worms, do no wrong,

Come not near our fairy queen!

A Midsummer Night's Dream,
William Shakespeare

THE FAIRY QUEEN'S RULES

1 Fairies must always be considerate to each other.

2 Damage to nature's treasures will not be tolerated.

3 Animals are our friends and cruelty to them is an offence.

4 Jeering, mocking and bullying others because of their pointed ears, large nose or flat feet is strictly forbidden.

5 Litter should never be dropped in the streets and must be recycled in every instance.

6 Any item stolen by a resident will instantly turn to dust.

7 Tricks played on others must be mischievous, never mean.

8 Fairies who leave the kingdom must return for the summer festivities or will be unable to return for seven years.

9 Fairies must NEVER lead a human to Fairyland.

10 The queen must be obeyed at all times.

The heralds have sounded their trumpets
and the gates of the enchanted castle
have been opened by the fairy guards.
Watch in wonder – it's the Fairy Queen!

★ *The Fairy Queen is waiting to greet you.*
Join Titania in the magnificent Throne Room
where she meets all her subjects and visitors.

★ *Titania loves parties. The highlight of the*
fairy year is the Midsummer Ball where
the fairies dance the night away.

★ *Each morning the Fairy Queen chooses a new*
gown in her Dressing Room. Then her favourite
flower fairy maids style her hair.

FAIRY MAGIC ZONE

To reveal the Fairy Queen on her throne, press the **SPACEBAR** on your keyboard.

To see the Fairy Queen sprinkle fairy dust, press the **UP** direction key on your keyboard.

Press the **DOWN** direction key to see Titania turn stone pillars into beautiful flowers.

The Fairy Queen

★

Prepare to
enter Fairyland.
MEET THE
MAGICAL QUEEN!

Magic and Mischief

Although they are playful creatures, fairies are also hard workers. Most of them do their best to make the world beautiful, but a few naughty fairies put all their effort into playing tricks on humans.

Magic Wands

Not all fairies carry wands, but those that do are careful not to lose them, as they can be dangerous in the wrong hands. The perfect wand is made from a hazel stick. The bark is cut away and a sparkling crystal is tied to the end. Then it's sprinkled with fairy dust to give it special powers.

FAIRY GODMOTHERS

Most children have a fairy godmother to watch over them, although she rarely shows herself. Cinderella was lucky enough to meet hers otherwise she would never have made it to the ball. Sleeping Beauty was even luckier – she had six fairy godmothers to make sure the wicked fairy didn't get her way! If you should come across your fairy godmother, make the most of it – fairy godmothers only have the power to help each person once!

Fairy Ointment

This is a mysterious potion that fairies apply to the eyes of their newborn babies. It helps them to see magic, which is never revealed to human eyes.

FOUR-LEAF CLOVERS

These tiny plants are very precious to fairies. They can be used to ward off bad spells. Humans consider them lucky too, so keep an eye out for one! The first leaf is said to bring hope, the second, faith and the third, love. The fourth leaf is for good luck.

Fairy Spades

These are smooth, slippery, black stones. When placed in water they are said to cure sick animals and humans.

Fairy Dust

A fairy always carries a bag of fairy dust. The secret ingredients are only known to the fairy queen and king, but it is thought that the dust falls from the moon and stars at night. It is usually gold or silver, but some flower fairies add ground petals to make it pink or purple. Fairy dust contains so much magic that it works magic on anything it touches.

Fairy Arrows

Arrows, or elf-bolts, are made from tiny pieces of flint. They were once used by fairies to scare off hunters, but today they are used to deliver love potions or fairy medicine to humans. Some wicked fairies use them to make farm animals sick if a farmer has upset them.

CHANGELINGS

Changelings are fairy children who have been swapped with human babies. They are usually bad-tempered, with a face a bit like an old man or woman. The only way to find out whether your brother or sister is a changeling is to serve them dinner in an egg shell. If they are fairy children they will cackle and speak as though they have lived for a hundred years. But don't worry, changelings are extremely rare!

House Fairies

Among all the fairies, the house fairies are probably the most useful to humans. There are those who are naughty and unhelpful but, for the most part, house fairies help with chores and look after the family. One thing these fairies have in common is the love of a clean house! They need to be treated well – insult one and things could start to go wrong around the home…

The Fairy Housekeeper

Mum and dad might notice the house looking extra clean, but they'd never suspect a fairy was at work! Each house has just one fairy housekeeper, who is helped by brownies and silkies. This fairy loves children and chooses a warm, loving home to stay in, particularly if mum is overworked. She loves strawberries and cream, and will be delighted if you leave out a gift for her.

Silkies

Silkies are pretty fairies who dress in white or grey silk dresses. In the old days, when people had servants to do their chores, silkies would scold those who were not doing a good job. Nowadays, silkies do the chores themselves to help busy families. They are useful to forgetful people too, as they lead them to lost items, such as keys. However, unlike brownies, they have a mischievous side, and like to jump out of trees to scare travellers!

Brownies

These helpful little sprites love housework. They are not the prettiest of creatures, with flat faces and lots of hair, but they have the most enchanting smiles and friendly characters. They love to play with children and any child lucky enough to meet a brownie will be entertained with wonderful stories. The only thing that will drive your brownie away is a gift left out for them. This insults their good nature and they will never return, so beware!

FAIRY FOOD

Nature provides all the food that fairies need – berries, fruit and honey. Fresh spring water helps to wash it down, although fairies that live on or near farmland love milk, straight from the cow. Fruit smoothies are a favourite treat, and for special occasions the fairies bake fairy cakes in a stone oven hidden in woodland caves.

A NAUGHTY HOUSE FAIRY

The boggart is an unwelcome visitor in any home. These gnome-like creatures are dirty, smelly and bad tempered. They often play nasty tricks, such as tipping over jugs or loudly slamming doors! Boggarts also tease dogs to make them bark. They are hard to get rid of, but will be chased away by banging pots and pans!

Garden Fairies

Of all the world's fairies, those found at the bottom of your garden are the smallest. Their tiny size means that they can live close to humans – grown-ups are far too busy to spot them. On the rare occasions they are spotted, it is usually by a child!

Fairy Gardeners

The fairies that tend garden flowers wake up very early to make sure the plants have enough dew. They check that the buds and blooms are coming through in the right colours, and can change them with fairy dust if they aren't quite right. They are very beautiful and dress in delicate outfits made from petals and leaves.

Pixies

Pixies are winged creatures with pointed noses and ears. They are very friendly, but do enjoy playing pranks on humans, such as making plants grow in funny directions! Pixies love to get together and dance at pixie fairs. You can sometimes see where they have met – look for shimmering footprints of pixie dust.

Farm Fairies

On the more practical land of a farm, the fairies are
very different from the delicate creatures of the garden. The farm fairies
are strong by nature and, therefore, able to help with the heavy work involved.
However, the delicate farm elf deals with more gentle farm chores.

Farmhands

Farmhand fairies ask only for a
glass of milk in return for help with
the farm work. The female, who
has flowing blonde hair, travels from
farm to farm to tend cattle.
As she travels by water, she
arrives at the farm door
soaking wet and asks to dry
herself by the fire. If she is
let in, she brings good
luck to the family!

Portunes

These tiny fairies look like
wrinkled old men! They are so
small they can get through locked
doors and appear in farmhouses at night
to roast frogs on the fire. They
have been known to annoy
people by leading horses
into marshes and bogs.

A Fairy Cobbler

The cheeky leprechaun is actually a fairy cobbler who
makes shoes for a living, but he is happy to help out on a farm.
He may give the farmer a good luck charm, such as a four-leaf clover.
In return he will ask the farmer to make him tiny furniture,
or give him leather for his shoes. Legend has it that if a human
is lucky enough to catch a leprechaun, he is led to the end of
the rainbow where a pot of gold awaits!

The Farm Elf

These are the smallest and the
prettiest of the farm workers. They can
be found helping milk turn to butter in the churn
and giving the cheese its beautiful rind. They also
like to look after the smaller farm animals, such
as the chicks and lambs, but they keep
well away from the farm cat!

A beautiful, fragrant garden is a sure sign
that a garden fairy has been hard at work.
Quietly creep up to a flowerbed and
see if you can spot her.

★ *Look closely and you might be lucky enough to
see a tiny garden fairy flying from flower to flower.*

★ *Garden fairies are always busy.
Looking after the flowers is their favourite job.*

★ *A little fairy magic helps a garden fairy
keep a garden full of bright flowers.*

FAIRY MAGIC ZONE

Press the **SPACEBAR** on your keyboard to open the flower and find the fairy inside.

To watch the fairy dust turn the flowers purple press the **UP** direction key.

To see the flowers turn red press the **LEFT** direction key.

To see the flowers turn pink press the **RIGHT** direction key.

To see the flowers turn yellow press the **DOWN** direction key.

The Garden Fairy

Enter the magical garden with care. **FRAGILE CREATURE INSIDE!**

Fairy Homes

For those who live in Fairyland, there is no problem finding the perfect home. However, for garden, woodland and water fairies, it can be more tricky.

House Hunting

Fairy homes need to be in a pretty place, hidden from inquisitive human eyes. They are always built in sheltered areas as fairies prefer not to get wet (unless they are water fairies, of course!). The places they choose must be clean, as fairies hate litter. Many a fairy has been forced to leave their home because of careless litterbugs.

Garden fairies build tiny homes from twigs and leaves. Woodland fairies prefer the hollow of a tree, or the inside of a large toadstool. You might find a fairy ring, which is a circle of toadstools, used by the tiniest woodland fairies.

Leprechauns often live in the cellars of houses or in the corner of a barn. Dream and tooth fairies always live in Fairyland, in sugar-pink houses around the chief tooth fairy's palace. Beautiful water fairies live in shimmering coral caves decorated with mother-of-pearl and seashells.

A Woodland Fairy's Home

Fairy carpenters carve bowls from oak branches. They are used to mix spells in.

Fairy lights are powered by fireflies, which are kept in a tiny cage.

Walnut shells are used to hold fairy dust and must be kept locked at all times!

Ancient fairy spell books are handed down through the generations.

Fairy carpenters make shelves from bark found on the forest floor.

Fairy Kitchens

Fairies love cooking for friends and family. They use small toadstools, or stones, as chairs and tables, and tiny plates and cups are made from nutshells.

Tiny toadstools can be used as a table and chairs.

Fairies do the washing up in a sink made from a conker shell.

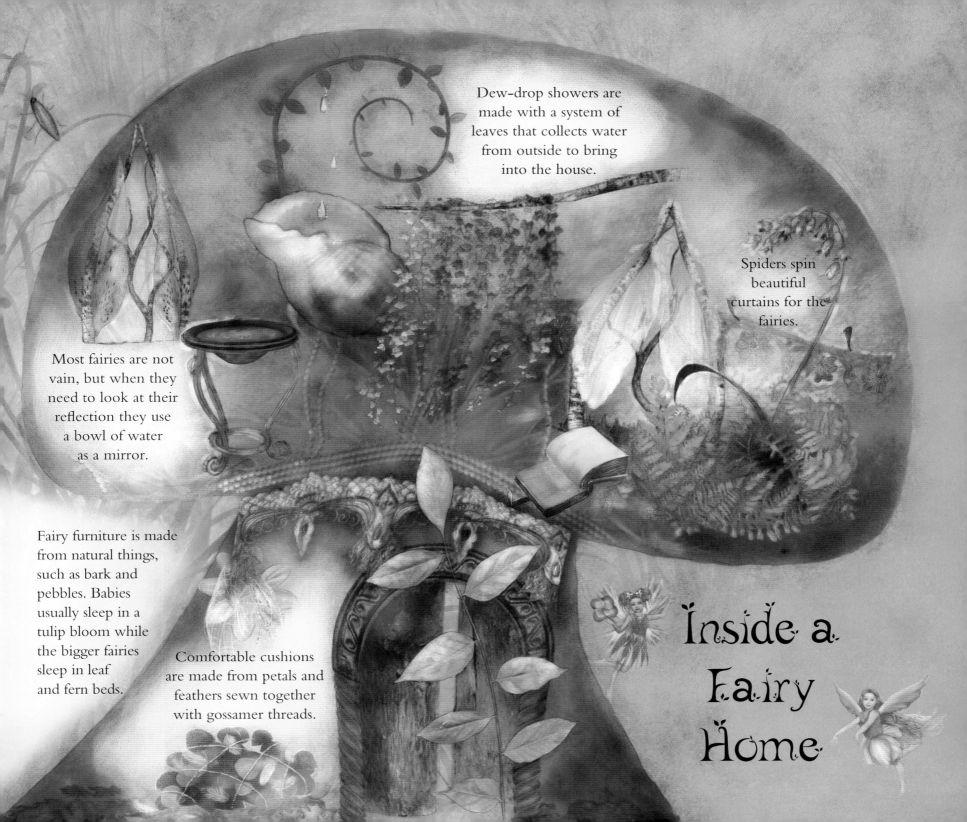

Dew-drop showers are made with a system of leaves that collects water from outside to bring into the house.

Spiders spin beautiful curtains for the fairies.

Most fairies are not vain, but when they need to look at their reflection they use a bowl of water as a mirror.

Fairy furniture is made from natural things, such as bark and pebbles. Babies usually sleep in a tulip bloom while the bigger fairies sleep in leaf and fern beds.

Comfortable cushions are made from petals and feathers sewn together with gossamer threads.

Inside a Fairy Home

Woodland Fairies

Forests and woods are perfect places for shy little fairy folk to hide in. Here, they are safe from the litter and noise of the human world, and from mortal eyes, especially those of the grown-ups.

Woodland fairies enjoy each other's company and love to get together to share secrets and gossip! At night they gather to talk and dance in the moonlight.

Gnomes

These wise guardians of mines and quarries are often found in forests. They love things that glitter, especially gem stones.

A Woodland Fairy's Day

8am: Breakfast at the big oak tree

9am: Collect seeds from bluebells and forget-me-nots

10am: Scatter seeds throughout the wood

1pm: Lunch

2pm: Collect petals

4pm: Make petal perfume

6pm: Find new ferns for beds

7pm: Home for dinner

10pm: Put on dancing shoes for the fairy meeting!

Wood Nymphs

These fairies live in trees and only live as long as their tree does. They are beautiful and kind, but get angry if their homes are damaged. Careful you don't break a branch when you climb a tree!

THE BLUEBELL FESTIVAL

The fairy Bluebell Festival is held in spring when the bluebells bloom. A beautiful carpet of flowers provides a lovely setting for the festival, and the little folk gather from miles around to celebrate. In shimmering dresses and best waistcoats, they dance away to mark the end of a long, cold winter.

BUTTERFLY FAIRIES

These rare fairies have colourful wings like butterflies. They live deep in the forest, feeding on nectar and honey. They are so shy, they are hardly ever seen.

Woodland Sprites

Sprites are usually found near streams or lakes. They can be mischievous, but are never spiteful. In autumn they paint the leaves different shades of yellow and red.

Work and Play

During the day, woodland fairies work hard, looking after flowers and trees, as well as animals. Squirrels and mice are their friends – they are happy to let tired fairies ride on their backs.

Woodland fairies love midnight picnics. They feast on nuts, acorns and blackberries – and honey! Pixies collect honey from bees, then take it to the woodland fairies.

What's that rustling among
the leaves on the forest floor?
Could it be a woodland fairy?
Tread softly and take a closer look.

★ *Wherever there are trees you're sure to find woodland fairies, but look carefully because they are very shy!*

★ *In summer the woodland fairies collect petals to make a beautifully scented perfume.*

★ *When winter is over and the bluebells appear the woodland fairies celebrate the arrival of spring.*

FAIRY MAGIC ZONE

- To see the woodland fairy fast asleep, press the **SPACEBAR** on your keyboard.

- Press the **UP** direction key to wake up the shy woodland fairy.

- To see the woodland fairy sound her flute, press the **DOWN** direction key.

The Woodland Fairy

Prepare to enter the enchanted forest. SHH! THE FAIRY IS ASLEEP!

Famous Fairies

When the name of a fairy is known throughout the world, the fairy queen grants him or her a place in the Fairyland Hall of Fame. This gallery contains portraits of famous fairies in history. The good ones get pride of place in the gallery, while the bad fairies' portraits hang in a dark corner.

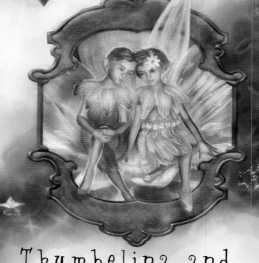

The Blue Fairy

If it wasn't for the beautiful Blue Fairy, Pinocchio, a mischievous little puppet, would never have become a real boy!

Brave Pinocchio! In return for your good heart I forgive you all your past misdeeds.

The Blue Fairy, Pinocchio, Carlo Collodi

The Christmas Fairy

The Christmas Fairy helps Santa create the lists of presents for each child. When the Christmas decorations go up, the Christmas Fairy leaves the North Pole and looks after Christmas trees all over the world. If she doesn't tend them, they might lose their needles before Christmas day!

Thumbelina and Tom Thumb

Thumbelina was a beautiful, tiny fairy child who was brought up by a human woman. Kidnapped by a frog who wanted a bride for her son, Thumbelina escaped with the help of a butterfly, but was then stolen away by a mayfly! She was finally delivered to a handsome fairy prince on the back of a bird.

Tom Thumb was also a fairy child, no bigger than a thumb. He was accident-prone and often fell into animal troughs, but he used magic to escape.

The Sleeping Beauty Fairies

Sleeping Beauty had six fairy godmothers who tried to protect her, but their sister, the wicked fairy, cast a spell that destined Sleeping Beauty to prick her finger on her sixteenth birthday, and die. One of the good fairies used her magic to soften the curse so that she wouldn't die, but would fall into a deep sleep for a hundred years. It was a hundred years before a handsome prince woke the princess with a kiss!

The Snow Queen

This fairy queen was bewitchingly beautiful, but she had a cold and wicked heart! Anybody who was kissed by her three times turned to ice.

Tinker Bell and Neverland

The most famous fairy of all, Tinker Bell, was Peter Pan's fairy. She was given her name because she fixed pots and kettles, like a tinker, and her voice sounded like a bell. She flitted about very quickly and appeared as a tiny light in the dark. She could be very bad-tempered, but was devoted to Peter and protected him from the evil Captain Hook.

The fur coat and the cap were made of snow, and it was a woman, tall and slender and blinding white – she was the Snow Queen herself.
The Snow Queen, Hans Christian Andersen

Second to the right and straight on till morning...
Peter Pan, J. M. Barrie

Water Fairies

Water has magical qualities
and attracts many types of fairy.
Whether they live in vast seas, tranquil lakes or
tiny streams, water fairies look after the plants,
fish and many other creatures that share
their underwater homes.

Asrai

Small and beautiful, Asrai fairies are hard to
spot as they are afraid of sunlight and are so
delicate you can see right through them! They live
in the deep blue seas and only come to the surface
on moonless nights, once every hundred years.

THE FISHERMAN AND THE ASRAI

Long ago, when a full moon shone bright, a fisherman pulled in his nets to find a beautiful creature
caught in the mesh. The Asrai begged him to
release her, but her voice sounded like the waves,
and he didn't hear. She pleaded with her eyes, but
the fisherman was greedy, and thought he could
make money from her.

When he reached the shore, the fisherman
gathered the townsfolk to take a look at his
beautiful captive. But when he moved the net, all
he found was a puddle of water. As the years went
by, whatever the weather, a spot on his arm where
the Asrai had touched him remained icy cold.

Water Sprites

These tiny fairies look like human females, but have hair as blue as the sea in which they live. They can breathe in both air and water, and are friendly unless threatened. They are happy to help humans in danger, and have been known to rescue fishermen who have fallen overboard.

THE LADY OF THE LAKE

You may have heard of King Arthur and his famous sword, Excalibur. It was given to him by the fairy known as the Lady of the Lake. A water fairy with vast powers, the Lady of the Lake gave the king the enchanted sword to protect him in battle. When he was finally wounded, Excalibur was thrown back into the misty waters and the Lady was seen rising from the water to reclaim it.

The Fin Folk

The Fin Folk, or Sea Gardeners, are tiny pixies who live in their own underwater paradise. They live mostly under the seas and oceans around the world, but are sometimes found in lagoons and saltwater lakes.

Gardening is the Fin Folk's favourite pastime and their kingdoms are full of brightly coloured flowers. These hardworking fairies spend all their waking hours tending underwater plants and wildlife and have special spells to protect them. Fin Folk can grow flowers of colours never seen in human gardens, such as silver and gold. They have even grown a rainbow rose, which has petals in the seven colours of the rainbow!

Only a few lucky people have ever caught sight of these beautiful underwater realms – a magical sight that is never forgotten!

Glastigs

Female water sprites, known as Glastigs, have the faces and bodies of beautiful women and the hooves of goats. These fairies love music and help women and children who are in trouble, but they can be dangerous to human men, luring them into traps with sweet music and dancing.

Water Nymphs

Beautiful water nymphs watch over fountains, springs, wells and streams. Each nymph stays with her own spring or stream, watering the land and helping plants to grow. These fairies can give water special healing powers. Those who drink from a fountain or well that is home to a water nymph soon find that good luck comes their way!

Ripples spreading across a lake could mean that a water fairy has just vanished below the surface. Meet the fairy that knows how to make a splash – the water fairy!

★ *Look beneath the glittering surface of water and you could catch a glimpse of a water fairy looking back at you.*

★ *Water fairies love to dive deep underwater to explore and to meet fish and other water creatures.*

★ *Some water fairies love to play jokes. So watch out when you're near water – they might splash you!*

FAIRY MAGIC ZONE

- To see the water fairy come out of the water, press the **SPACEBAR** on your keyboard.

- Press the **UP** direction key to watch the wonderful water fairy hover.

- To make her sit sit on the rock, press the **DOWN** direction key.

The Water Fairy

Approach the shimmering pond with caution. **YOU MAY GET SPLASHED!**

The Tooth Fairy

One of the busiest of all the fairies is the tooth fairy. Every time a wobbly baby tooth falls out, she knows about it and, no matter where in the world it is, she will be there to collect it that night…

Collecting Teeth

The tooth fairy always leaves a coin or a gift behind in return for a tooth. The teeth she collects are kept in a huge store room at her palace. A special assistant works in the tooth library where the names of all the children in the world are kept. Fairies travel from far and wide to buy the gorgeous jewellery that the tooth fairy's elf friends make from teeth.

The tooth fairy is one of the prettiest of fairies. She wears shimmering white gowns and jewellery made from the purest of baby teeth. Her pearl slippers are made of spun white silk. She carries a gold silk purse full of fairy dust. If a child stirs while she is collecting her treasures, she sends him or her back to sleep with just a pinch of the dust.

Travelling the World

How does the tooth fairy know where she is needed every night? During the day, while the tooth fairy sleeps, sprite spies travel the world looking for children with wobbly teeth. If it looks like a tooth's about to pop out, the sprites write the child's name in a special book.

The tooth fairy checks the names in the book and works out her collection round for the night ahead.

The Dream Fairies

Dream fairies work only at night and sleep during the day. Their job is to banish nightmares and to make sure that children are tucked up in bed and have sweet dreams. If they come across a child having a bad dream, they take the dream away and blow it up to the skies, where it forms a small black cloud. The small clouds join together to make a big heavy cloud, then the nightmares are turned into rain, washing all bad thoughts away.

SWEET DREAMS

★ Always go to bed when your parents tell you – don't keep the dream fairies waiting!
★ Think lovely thoughts as you put your head on the pillow. Holidays, beaches and best friends are perfect dreamy thoughts.
★ It's a good idea to say "Goodnight dream fairies". They love to be welcomed into a room!

Fairy Foes

Most fairies put their magic to good use, but they have to be very careful as they have some enemies. The creatures that possess similar magical powers to the good fairies, but use them for wicked purposes, pose the greatest danger. The worst among these are the witches, goblins and trolls who do their best to spoil the fairies' good work.

Witches

These cave-dwelling hags often live in woodland where fairies live – and oh, how they hate them! They use their magic to trap fairies, imprisoning them in bottles so they can steal their fairy dust. A pinch of fairy dust added to a witch's cauldron makes her spell twice as powerful. Really wicked witches have been known to put a whole fairy in the pot if she refuses to hand over her dust!

However, some witches have come to see the error of their ways after meeting a particularly good fairy. These "white witches" can use their spells to help others.

THE FROST GIANTS

The frost giants live in Niflheim, a land of eternal cold, and are the enemies of the elves and fairies.

The first frost giant was called Ymer and was formed when the cold air of Niflheim met the warm air of the neighbouring land of fire and embers. As Ymer slept his body grew in size and a whole race of giants was born.

The giants can freeze everything for miles around and use their powers to destroy the marine life, plants and flowers that fairies work so hard to protect. They often take the form of a freezing fog to move across the land, destroying wildlife in their path. The layer of frost left on objects after a freezing fog could mean that a giant has passed that way. They rarely harm humans, though – for one thing they would melt if they entered a human house!

Goblins

...hobgoblins, these stocky ... the fairies. They are so ...ttier fairy races and ...eous babies with ...y hate elves ... meet. A go... ...magic ca...

Trolls

Fairies are very frightened of the ugly ogre-like creatures that guard the bridges of the hills and mountains. Trolls are usually green in colour and, although they eat goats, they are unlikely to harm people, preferring to scare them instead. They dislike fairies and will squash them with their huge hands if they get the chance. Luckily most fairies are too quick for these stupid, lumbering creatures and manage to escape.

Finding Fairies

You may have fairies at the bottom of your garden or even in your house, but they use magic to hide. If you are very lucky, though, you might find clues that a fairy has left behind. Children are much better at spotting these signs than grown ups.

In the House

A drop of milk or some breadcrumbs in the kitchen could mean that fairies have been having a meal. If your cat is very interested in something under the cupboard, or the dog seems restless, it could be because they have seen a fairy. If an animal starts chasing its tail, it may be because it has an invisible rider!

In the Garden

Look under the bushes in the garden and see if you can find a pile of leaves or petals. A fairy may have slept there. A row or a circle of stones can mean a midnight meeting has taken place, as they are often used as seats.

FAIRY RINGS

At night, fairies have been spotted dancing in woodland where they leave small circles known as fairy rings. Never search for these night-time dances on your own – their magic is very powerful. The enchanting music tempts people to come too close. People who have been lured have told strange stories of how the dance seemed to last only for a few moments, but in fact had lasted for seven years!

In the Woods

The most obvious sign that fairies are living in the woods is a ring of toadstools. If you find a hollow tree, take a peek inside. Any piles of leaves, acorns or twigs may well have been left there by fairies.

ATTRACTING FAIRIES

The best time to attract good fairies is when the moon is full. This is a very magical time.

Some flowers have special properties. Sunflowers, nasturtiums and tulips are fairy favourites, likely to bring them near. Fruits, such as strawberries, provide them with food, while sweet-smelling flowers, such as lavender and honeysuckle, can attract fairies from further away. Building a fairy house and leaving tiny cups of water inside is a lovely way to make fairies feel welcome.

The best possible way of attracting house fairies is to keep everything clean! Untidy bedrooms will have these fairies scooting off into the night, and dust and dirt will only attract bad fairies.

A rustle in the wind reminds us a fairy is near...

Shh! You may frighten the fairies away.
Tiptoe nearer, keep a close watch
and who knows, you
might just catch a fairy...

★ *To find a fairy you need to tune in*
to your senses. A sudden, quiet breeze
could mean one is very near...

★ *Fairies love to dance at fairy rings in the woods, so*
keep your eyes open when you're out for a walk!

★ *Fairies always hide from grown-ups. They*
are usually very shy, but they do love
nice children who are fairy friends.

FAIRY MAGIC ZONE

- Take the disc out of the envelope and hold it in your hand.

- Press the **SPACEBAR** on your keyboard to offer a goblet of water.

- To tempt the fairy with luscious fruit, press the **UP** direction key.

- To attract the fairy with flower petals, press the **DOWN** direction key.

- To make the fairy finally appear, press the **RIGHT** and **LEFT** direction keys together.

To Catch a Fairy

Prepare to meet a fairy.
**HOLD YOUR
HAND OUT
GENTLY!**

Fairy Fashions

Fairies are very fashion conscious and love to look their best, especially at their nightly meetings. Using spider silk, colourful petals and pretty leaves, fairies are very creative at making clothes and jewellery from nature's treasures.

Nature's Treasures

Spider silk is the most beautiful and delicate material, and is in plentiful supply in woods, gardens and houses. Spiders are happy to spin it for their fairy friends. Ants, bees and wasps are also able to make silk, which they use for nest-building. A fairy who helps busy insects collect nectar will be rewarded with the rarest of silk, which is normally saved for making ball gowns.

Petals and leaves are often used for fairy outfits, particularly those of the flower and woodland fairies. Fairies always have a sparkling new outfit for for the midsummer celebrations, which take place on the longest day of the year.

ACCESSORIES

Brightly coloured fairy jewellery is made from dried seeds and berries, or from gems and crystals which are mined by the elves. Water fairies make their trinkets from coral and pearls, and they love mother-of-pearl shells with their swirling colours of silver and pink.

For footwear, the fairies rely mainly on leprechauns, the fairy cobblers. Leprechauns sew the daintiest shoes as well as make the sturdy boots that elves wear. Silk is used for bags and crushed petals provide coloured dye for the fabric. Bags and hats are made from petals, as well as walnut and hazelnut shells. Colourful feathers make charming additions to the hats.

FAIRY WINGS

In Fairyland, wings are very fashionable but not all fairies are born with them. Flightless fairies often possess several pairs of wings which they wear for special occasions. These are spun from the finest gossamer and are attached to threads which can be tied over the shoulders. Wings are also made from feathers, shed by young birds as they learn to fly.

Seasonal Dressing

In order to stay hidden, fairies try to blend into the background. Many types, particularly woodland fairies, change their clothing to reflect the changing seasons.

Autumn

As leaves and petals fall from the trees in shades of red, green and orange, the elf tailors make them into autumn outfits. Acorn shells lined with soft feathers make comfortable hats and fallen conker shells are used to make umbrellas.

Spring

As nature awakens in a riot of blue and green, the fairies celebrate by sewing beautiful ball gowns in preparation for the Bluebell Festival. Tulip pink, daffodil yellow and, of course, bluebell blue are the colours of the season!

Winter

White spider silk and rabbits' hair are woven together to make warm coats for the fairies and blankets for the babies. Farm fairies and those that live near sheep collect tufts of wool from the fences and bushes; these are woven into felt to line their boots. Ivy-leaf shawls are popular for eveningwear at this time of year.

Summer

As this is the most colourful season of the year, fairies take the opportunity to dress in vibrant pinks and purples, to echo the many blooming flowers. Their outfits are skimpy at this time of year, as they do not like to be too hot, and they often wear petal sunhats.

Certificate of Fairyland

This is to certify that

....

Place your
photograph
here

is now a keeper of fairy secrets.

From this day forth, by royal command, she shall be recognized
as a trusted friend of fairy folk and will swear never to
reveal her knowledge to the grown-up ones.

Queen Titania